Ducks in a Row...Short Stories
By: Eddie J. Martin

Fictional lockup, Way to Heaven, Love in, Love out and Pussy Whipped.

For: Ronald Chaison,

My friend and confidant. Who's been there for me

faithfully for over 20 years. You're the best!

LOCKUP:

If only doing time was really this easy, everyone would want to try it.

Way to heaven:
Is there a guaranteed way to heaven, even for a

hitman?

Love in, Love out:
Love only comes around once, have you used

yours up?

Pussy Whipped:

Sweet Jennings was knocking them out left and
right and no one could stand up to him, that is
until he met Pussy.

Other books by this author:

Enlisted at 14

Enlisted at 14 and the Journey Continues

Willow... A novel

Just a Dream

Willow... and the Medusa

Enlisted at 14... Looking back

Meet Ruben Kane

Willow... One for the Team

R.K. {Ruben Kane}

Ruben's Bag

Little Miss Willow....A Short Story

Smooth...A Ruben Kane Novel

Ruben's Bad Side

Fictional Lockup

Part 1

The bus stopped outside the prison gate. I don't know about the rest of the guys, but I was shaking in my boots. This was my first time going to the big house. Although I've been to local jails, I've heard this is a big step and nothing like what I've been used to. The barbed wire and the guards—twice as many as there were in the local jails. The building was at least ten stories high and the noise could be heard from where we were on the bus. This was no good. I don't know what I was thinking, but it surely wasn't this. I've heard the guys on the street talk about it, but they sounded like it was a rite of passage. I haven't even walked into the place and could tell right away I wanted no part of it; yet, here I am with five years to do. This is no good!

If I hadn't gotten into that last altercation, I wouldn't be here, but what could one do? A sucker comes up to you and feels your ass, like you're some punk or something. You have no choice; you have to do something. If the word got around that he did that you have to act. As they say, fuck or fight, maybe I do a little fucking, but I'm not getting fucked!

The bus pulled inside the gate and we were all ordered off. We stood outside the bus as they unchained us and listening to bullshit as to what we can and can't do. I was hearing and I wasn't hearing. I looked at the others and they had a couple of junior flips that were more shook up than me. The way I saw was that the older guys would focus more on them than me, although I had already decided I was going to fight, had to fight; win or lose, that's just the way it is.

We all walked into the building and took off all our clothes, showing our asses and sticking out our tongues. We changed into prison dress and were assigned a cell. I had a two-man cell and my cellmate was a small guy, about 5 foot 2, one hundred and 20 pounds with a very high voice. As soon as I walked into the cell, he annoyed me. I had a feeling I wouldn't be here that long.

A year ago, I was out in the country just seeing the sites and finishing off a filth of tequila. My girl and I had just got into a fight about another female—some woman she heard about. She was right, but what the hell, things are like that sometimes. One thing led to another and I ended up hitting her upside the head. The cops were called, I left before they arrived and I ended up in the country knocking out this jug. I had a feeling that when they caught up to me, I'd be doing some hard time, with being on probation and the judge telling me she didn't want to see me again. There was no way of getting around it.

I ended up at a private fishing hole that I knew of— a creek running through, with a small open space. I had to walk a ways to get to it but as I did, I noticed a craft of some kind hidden by some trees. If I didn't know any better, I'd say it was a spacecraft. I hesitated for a second, then the tequila told me to get a little closer and check it out. Before I moved, I took a long hit of the bottle and said out loud, "Fuck it!" and started walking toward the craft. It was round-shaped and silver with lights all around it, just like what you see in the movies. It was about twelve feet around, with a glass canopy on top. I tried looking inside but saw nothing but gauges, and not a damn seat to sit down on. I was wondering how one could get inside this thing when out of the corner of my eye, I saw some movement. I turned to see what it was and saw it was a kid, or what I thought was a kid. It had all the characteristics of a kid—it was about 5 foot, one hundred pounds, had a large head and extra-large eyes but no eyebrows or hair on its head or face. It didn't have a nose or lips, there was just a hole where the mouth should be. It had two short arms and legs, and long fingers, but only three on each hand and no thumbs. It also had some of the biggest feet I've ever seen; it would have given Shaquille O'Neal a run for his money. For clothes, it had on a one-piece jumpsuit that looked like it was poured on him. It went up to its neck. It also had a medallion hanging from a long chain around its neck with a symbol I'd never seen before. It looked at me and I looked at it.

"You are not afraid of me?" it said. I don't know how it could talk out of that small hole in its mouth.

So, I took a drink and said, "You're not afraid of me?" By this time, I'm high as hell and I was fearing no one.

"Most of you people who see me are afraid and run away or try to harm me," it said. "But I see you are quite different."

"You got that right, Mr. Is this your ride?" I asked, referring to the spacecraft.

"If you are referring to Raun, yes, it is my spacecraft."

"Who are you and where did you come from?" I asked. "Not from around here, I gather?"

"No, I'm not from your planet. I stop here on my way to another one but you people are not too friendly," it said. "I'm from a solar system a few light years away from here called Vane. Once a year, we come by this way just to check on your progress."

"We?" I said. "There's others like you?"

"Yes," it said. They're with the mothership outside the stratosphere."

"What are you checking this planet for, seeing if we've been good or bad?" I said.

"That's close to being correct," it said. "You are very intelligent, although we already knew you were, but you still do unintelligent things."

"So, you're grading us?" I asked. "How are we doing?"

"Not too good, I'm sorry to say. We've been monitoring this planet for hundreds of years. It was beautiful once but within the last 100 to 150 years, it has, as you people would say, 'gone to the dogs'. My people are very disappointed in you but since it's your world, we've been willing to look the other way, except now, you want to leave your world and bring all this mayhem to the rest of the universe, and we can't have that."

"So, what are you planning on doing?" I asked. "Destroy the whole world?"

"If we have to," it said. "You understand we can't let you keep going the way you're going. I'm sorry," it said, "but I have to go. I'm a little behind schedule now. Maybe we can meet here again next year?"

"Yeah, maybe we can," I said. "Say, I don't even know your name."

"Call me Centrale," it said.

As it was getting into its ship, it asked if it could hold my hand. Reluctantly, I said yes and when I did, I felt a small electrical charge go through me. I pulled my hand back and asked, "What was that?"

"That is a communication wave my people use. Whenever you need to contact me, just rub your left hand three times with your right and we can communicate between us. Now, I must go. Goodbye my friend!"

Centrale entered the craft, and it lifted off the ground with only a whisper of a sound. I took another huge drink and watched it fly out of sight. I sat down by an old oak tree and thought about what just happened. I felt a little tingle on my left hand, then fell off to sleep.

The police woke me up a few hours later, and not too gently. They all had their guns pointing at me, then turned me over and put handcuffs on me. They picked me up off the ground and forced me to stand up. I looked down at what was left of my jug and asked them if I could finish it off.

"Sure," one of them said. So, picked it up and held it towards me and then tossed it in the creek. "Now, get your ass moving," he said.

Later, I wondered how the cops found me, then remembered I had brought my girlfriend here once and told her this would be "our place". The county jail was my next stop, and since I didn't have bail money, I sat there for six months. I convinced my girlfriend not to press charges but the district attorney wasn't having any of it and felt I needed a lesson since I was on parole and all, and the judge agreed with him. It didn't help that when I was in county jail, I bust some guys head open because he tried to grab my junk while I was asleep. Last I heard, he was in a coma! The judge didn't understand that I didn't want to have a man touching my junk. What would the other inmates think? Nevertheless, they placed me in solitary confinement until I went to trial and again, I opened my big mouth when the judge sentenced me to three years, with five years' probation. By this time, I had spent two months in the hole and wasn't in the best of moods, so I said to the judge, "Fuck you! Why not make it five years and 10 years' probation?" So, he did, and advised me to keep my mouth shut, then told me to have a nice day.

Two weeks later, I was on the prison bus headed upstate. For a few weeks, my cellmate and I got along pretty well, and even though I had my doubts about him, I liked the little guy. One afternoon at lunch, one of the prison bullies started on him about giving over part of his canteen goods for protection (canteen goods are a form of currency). He even came to our cell and threatened him. So, naturally, there I was (big brother) and bigmouth. I had to take up for my cellmate. The bully and I got written up and we were given 30 days in solitary confinement. I tried to explain the situation to the officers, but they wanted to hear none of it. In their minds, if one threw a punch and the other threw a punch, then were both fighting. So, I said, "Fuck you guys, why not give me 45 days?" So, they did!

I was placed in a one room cell, with no windows. It had one thin mattress and one army blanket. I was allowed one shower a week and one hour outside the cell in the yard each day. By the second week, I began to realize that maybe I had made a big mistake. There was absolutely nothing to do except look at the four walls, maybe do some push-ups, play with myself, and think of all the shit I did wrong and how I could have done it differently. On that 30th day, the day I should have been getting out, I was really going up the walls. A weak man would have shed a few tears. But not me; not yet anyway! On my 35th day in the hole, the guard brought my lunch and I kicked it back outside the vent in which it came in. I did that three to four times and I must admit that after a while, I got a little hungry. Nevertheless, they tacked 30 more days on top the 45 I already had. When the committee put that on me, I asked, "How am I supposed to do 30 more days? I can't do the time I've got now."

The one lady just looked at me and said, "Do the best you can, Mr. Chandler." Then she told me to have a nice day. On my 45th day of being in the hole, I knew this was it; I knew I couldn't make it another day. Tomorrow, I promised myself, I'd plead—no, beg—to be released. At 2 o'clock that afternoon, they came to get me and take me to the yard for that hour. In the yard, in my private cage, with no one to talk to I did my usual thing. I ran around for 20 minutes, played basketball for another 25, and did the sign language thing with the other inmates for the rest of the time to find out what was going on outside the hole. When the guards came back to get me, I was pretty much tuckered out, so when I entered my cell, I headed straight for my bunk. I closed my eyes and just laid there. I started thinking about how I got captured and remembered Centrale, the alien from another planet, and the whole episode and the conversation we had. Since I was drinking a lot that day, I chalked it all up to a bad dream and alcohol. After all, nothing like that could have really happened. But I remembered that before he had left, he took my hand and I received a small charge that went from his hand to mine. He told me that if I ever wanted to contact him, all I had to do was rube my left hand three times. "That's bullshit," I said to myself. "That had to be a dream." I smiled to myself and said, "Yeah, only a dream." However, I sat up in my bunk and looked at my left hand. What did I have to lose? I began to rub the inside of my palm three times. After about twenty seconds, Centrale came into my mind.

"Yes, John?"

At that point, I stood up and said, "Centrale, is that you?"

"Yes, it is I, John. It's been a long time. You were not at the place where we first met, were you detained?"

"You could say that, Centrale. Why you didn't call me?" I said.

"It doesn't work that way, John. It's a one-way line. You must call me, then we can communicate. It's complicated."

"But I'm hearing you in my head," I said. "How is that possible?"

"Again, it's complicated and it'll take longer than you want to spend talking about it. Where have you been, John? I thought you'd call me before now."

"Well, to tell you the truth, Centrale, I'm incarcerated, in jail, in the hoosegow."

"I understand what incarcerated means. What did you do to get incarcerated?"

"Like you said, Centrale, it's really a long story but I'm in this one-room cell that has nothing but a bed and a toilet in it, and I've been here over 40 days now."

"How long would you have to stay in such a place, John?"

"Five years or more, Centrale."

"That's a long time, John. What can I do to help?"

"I could use something to stimulate my mind while I'm here, like a book or something."

"That's rather easy to do, I'll just send you to one of your libraries and you just pick the book you want and start reading it."

"You will have to explain that to me, I am incarcerated you know."

"You'll get there through your mind and you'll read the book through your mind, and even turn the pages. Leave it to me, just lay back and we'll pick a library for you and you'll do the rest with your mind. You'll walk in the library, pick a book and return to your cell. When you finish, you'll return the book."

"Won't the guards see the book?" I asked. No one can see the book because it'll be in your head, but you can pull it up whenever you like."

Part 2

After talking to Centrale, I decided to try out what he had said, so I laid back on my bunk, put my hands behind my head and let my mind do the walking. I closed my eyes and within a minute, I could see myself walking into the New York public library. I stood at the door and looked around. There was nothing but books wherever I looked. And the goons here wouldn't even see fit to give me just one. I thought that at first, I'd look around and then pick a book. Centrale didn't say how many books I could pick, so I thought I'd just start with one. Crime, fiction, mystery, love? Not love; I'm suffering enough. They were all there, James Patterson, John Griffin, Toni Morrison,

Maya Angelo, Walter Mostly and James Baldwin. I decided on a John Grisham. I picked it out and went to the inside cover just by thinking about it. After looking around, I headed for the front door. Once I passed the entrance, I found myself back in my bunk. It was then that the guards brought my lunch. A ham and cheese sandwich, a small carton of milk, applesauce and a banana. Not much but what can you expect for prison food? After I finished my lunch, I decided to read my book. As soon as I thought about it, the book came into view and I started reading. Up until the time I received my book, I was giving the guards all kinds of hell. I was shaking the cell doors, calling them all kinds of names, and throwing shit at them—whatever. In turn, they would just add more time on me. I just never learned. But in my defense, I had literally nothing to do but fuck with the guards. But once I got the book, things changed. I stopped harassing my guards, I took my meals like I was supposed to and when they looked in on me, I was always laying on my bunk, sometimes laughing to myself. After a week or two of this, the guards got together and mentioned what a changed individual I was. They believed that the hole must have really changed me. That, or I was going cuckoo. Two weeks and five books later, two guards were passing my cell and discussing a new TV show that was on the night before. They said the ratings were through the roof. I started thinking, if Centrale could get me books, why not a TV? It sounded reasonable to me, so I did the hand thing—rubbed my palm three times—and Centrale answered.

"Yes, John?"

I told Centrale what I wanted and he told me I could have had a TV weeks ago, if I only asked.

"Close your eyes and call for your TV just like you did for your books and it'll be there. When you want to change stations, just will it to do so, just like changing the pages in a book. I almost fucked up one day when one of the guards stopped by and comminuted on how my attitude had changed in the last few weeks and then he happened to mention the new show and said I should watch it once I was out and I said, "Oh, I saw the show; it wasn't all that good."

He looked at me and said, "How the hell could you watch the show when you're in here looking at these four walls? We need to get you out of here, John. I think you've had it. How long have you got to go now?" he asked.

"Thirty more days," I said.

"Isn't that what you originally started with six months ago?"

"Yeah, I guess I just like it here," I said.

"Well, you're taking it a lot better than a lot of the inmates."

One night, I was watching TV and a commercial came on about a steakhouse food chain. Steak, potatoes and the trimmings. That food sure looked good and I haven't had a steak in a very long time. The way they make the food in those commercials look, it's like it's the best thing in the world, and after this prison food, anything would look good.

I would call Centrale in the morning. I don't know why I worry about the time I call him. I don't believe he's on any kind of timeframe. I think I'll just keep him on my time; it'll keep me straight anyway. The next morning after breakfast, I called Centrale.

"Yes John," he said.

"Let me ask you something," I said. "The food I get in here is for the dogs, and I would like to get something just a little better. Do you think you could arrange that?"

"No problem, John. Just tell me what you desire and I'll have it transported to where you are."

"Really?" I said. "Suppose I said I wanted a lobster from Maine?"

"I would search the best restaurants in Maine and would send you the dinner you requested," he said. "And to keep a low profile, I would transport your dishes back to that same restaurant."

"Damn," I said. "You can do all that? Why didn't you tell me that before?"

"You didn't ask, John," he said.

"Well, look Centrale. Since you can do all that, how about getting me out of this cell for a few hours?"

"I can do that, John. Just tell me where you want to go, for how long, and when. Eight hours is your max, John. And there is one other thing. I cannot bust you out of their permanently; our law forbids it, but I can do what I said I could."

"That's great, Centrale. Let's start with the lobster from Maine tonight and then we'll go from there."

Now, you tell me what kind of luck this is. I was in the hole and getting all this thrown at me. My only problem was to figure out a way to spend the rest of my time there. I knew where the first place I would ask Centrale to send me to would be—my old stomping ground to get laid. That'll knock out that first trip. While I was in the hole, I had my routine down pat: Breakfast at 6, lunch at 11, the yard at 3, and dinner at 5. All the other inmates in the hole had nothing to look forward to except the next day of doing nothing. I, however, would watch a little of the morning games shows and early morning news after breakfast, then read a chapter or two of my latest book after lunch, and after my hour in the yard, I would come back and take a little nap and wait for dinner of which I ate very little, anticipating my evening dinner from Centrale. And then, after all that, my night out on the town with Irma. Damn, I need to be in the hole if only to regroup.

My first trip out included cold chicken, milk, a bottle of vodka, eggs, cakes and a baked ham. I took the chicken and the vodka out of the refrigerator and placed it on the kitchen table, retrieved a cup out of the cabinet, poured the vodka to the top and drank it. I drank the vodka down in one hit. The light came on and there was Irma, standing in the doorway with a baseball bat in her hand.

"John?" she said and ran over to me and grabbed me. We both fell onto the floor and that's when she began to kiss me. We stayed there and made love for the next two hours. As we lay on the floor, with her still all over me, that's when the questions began. What was I doing there? Was I let out or did I break out? How did I get there?

She said she tried to visit but they told her I was in the hole and could not have any visitors or receive or write any letters. She said that for a while, she thought I was dead and she asked them if I was.

I wondered how much I should tell the old girl, after all, she's partly the reason I'm in there. Then, I thought, "What the hell, she probably won't believe it anyway." So, I told her the whole story—from the time I met Centrale to when I arrived there.

She just stared at me and said, "No way!"

I'll be gone at 5 o'clock," I said. "You remember the old Star Trek movies? When the guy says, 'Beam me up, Scotty'? That's kind of like what will happen to me."

"And you'll return tomorrow night, right?"

"Yes," I said. "I think!"

"Well, whatever, John. As long as you are here with me."

For the next few weeks, life was good until the day came for my release. I had to have my last meeting with the board members to approve it, and that's when I got kind of shaky. If they let me out of the hole and put me back into the population, I was fucked—I would be a regular inmate. I would go back to the funky old three meals a day in a 9 x 10 cell, with maybe two inmates. No, this is not looking good. What the hell can I do to stay where I am? Then, it occurred to me: the same thing that got me in here could keep me here. The three-person panel that socked it to me before were here again—two women and one man. The woman that gave me the hardest time the last time looked at me and smiled, knowing she had won.

"John, we've been hearing good things about you the last few months. Are you about ready to get out of here and return to the population?"

The two others shook their head in agreement, then the first judge said, "Yes, you've been great, John. We're ready to let you go today. What do you think about that?"

I looked at each one of them individually and said, "With all due respect, ladies and gentlemen, I only have one thing to say. Fuck you, fuck you, everyone." Then, I kicked the desk they were sitting behind, stood up and slapped the guard that was standing behind me and put a three-inch gash under his left eye. By the time they got me under control, I had done as much damage as I could, including jumping over the desk at the three judges. I guess they had decided there was no need to restrain me because they were going to let me go anyway. Big mistake! I almost got to that one bitch of a judge who was doing all that smiling. I managed to get to her blouse and ripped it down to her waist. Surprise, surprise, she didn't have a bra on. I took an ass kicking that day, a bad ass kicking, but I manage to get two years in the hole for it. Two years of living large! Just what I wanted!

I must say, things went beautifully for almost eightteen months. I hadn't heard from the committee again but I had heard rumors as to what happened after my incident. Apparently, someone took a picture of that one judge with her tits hanging out and it wound up all over the prison yard. She left and never came back. I heard she even left the prison system altogether. I must say, she did have some nice tits.

Six months before I was due to be released, I was over in Hawaii and I happened to run into one of the guards who worked on one of the upper tiers of the prison, but she knew about me. She spotted me right away and came over to me.

"John? John Chandler?" she said. "When did you get out?"

"I'm afraid you have the wrong person," I said. "I don't know a John Chandler."

"You know, you look just like a guy that's in our prison where I work. Do you have a brother that's incarcerated?"

"No, I'm afraid not, but you know what they say?" I said. "Everyone has a double in life. Well, gotta go," I said.

A week later, one of the guards passed my cell and asked me, smiling, if I had been to Hawaii lately.

"I don't think so," I said. "But when I do, I'll be sure to let you know."

"Listen to this, John," he said. "One of the guards on E-Row says she could have sworn she saw you on the beach in Hawaii. Ain't that a bitch?"

"Yeah, it is. How would I ever get from the hole to Hawaii? I'd have to be transported by a beam for that."

On Valentine's Day, officer Rogers passed my cell and wanted to fuck with me. There are some good guards and there are some downright dogs. This one was a good guy on Mondays, Tuesdays, and Wednesdays, and a dog on Thursdays and Fridays. This was a Thursday.

"Hey John, just wanted you to know that I got me some pussy last night. You know it being Valentine's Day and all, shoo was good. And guess what, John? We did it doggy style."

"Thanks for sharing that with me, Officer Rogers," I said. "I won't forget it."

"Anything for you, John. Anything to make your life a little easier."

"Asshole," I said.

"Watch your mouth, John. That remark could add more time in the hole for you."

One night, I decided not to go to Irma's because she'd been screwing my ass down and I needed a break, so I asked Centrale to send me to Tijuana, Mexico. That'll be a good trip and at midnight, that's about the right time. I like tequila and they have the good stuff there, with the worm in the bottom of the bottle and all.

On Friday night, the streets of Tijuana were full of people. Cars could hardly get by, and there was barely any room to walk on the sidewalks. The solicitors outside the clubs were begging you to come in their establishments, advertising topless girls.

The first place I went into, I ordered a double tequila. You know that's funny? When I asked

Centrale about money, he told me not to worry and said all I had to do was reach into my pocket and I would have the currency of the country I was in. I took him at his word and reached in my pocket and there it was. I even got change back. The bar I was in had topless girls dancing on the stage behind the bar, and I must admit, despite laying up with Irma a few nights a week, I still got horny. At around two in the morning and a lot of tequila later, I caught the eye of a fine young dancer. We planned to meet after the show. I stumbled to the back alley to the rear door of the club and waited for her. Instead of the girl showing up, three young men between 18 and 22 showed up. I must admit, they beat me down pretty good and took the few dollars I had left in my pocket. I think they would have hurt me even worse had the police not come along. The damnedest thing is, the kids got away and they took me to jail for disturbing the peace. The magistrate said that since it was a Friday night, it would be Monday before I got to see anyone to get me out. It was 3:30 at this point. They asked me if I had any money, and I looked at them and laughed.

"I've just been robbed, judge. I don't have a dollar."

"Well, that's too bad," the judge said. "The next bus that's headed for the main jail is at 6 o'clock this morning. In the meantime, we'll put you in the cells in the back. It's a lot better than what you'll be going to."

Another hour and a half and I'll be out of here, unless Centrale drops the ball and doesn't transport me back. I wouldn't want to spend a lot of time in a Mexican jail. From what I've heard, this is not the place to be, especially for an Anglo. There were three drunk Mexicans in the cell and one asked me, "Amigo, you got a cigarette for me?"

"Hell, no," I said. "I ain't got no damn cigarette for you." Since I was leaving, I knew I could talk tough.

An hour later, I was back in my own bunk, hungover, with sore ribs, and my nose felt like it was broken. I was beaten to hell. Now, I needed to hide it from the guards. I'll just tell them that I'm sick. If they ask me if I need to see the nurse, I'll just tell them I'll get over it in the next few days. And I did.

Part 3

I learned a lesson from that last trip to Mexico: no more topless bars for me, and no trying to get drawls other than Irma's. On these trips, I should just play it cool and mind my own business. After all, I've got everything that a guy in prison would ever want. I think I should work on getting my ass out of here, this night outing is fine but I would like to get out during the day sometime. I feel like a damn vampire!

One night, I was sitting on a bench off the lake on E. River Dr. in Chicago, about two in the morning, just watching the water and the skylight of downtown. No one was out at that time of morning but me. Or so I thought. I was wrong! A lady jogger came a ways down the walkway. I thought it was a lady because of her ponytail that was swinging in the wind but in today's world, you never know. Now, why would a lady be out jogging at this time in the morning? Some men would say, "She's just asking for it." Just as I thought that, a person jumped out of the bushes and attacked her. He pulled her into the shrubbery and started molesting her. Now, when I first saw this, my reaction was to jump up and run to her aid, but then I stopped. Every time I have ever tried to help someone, I was the one who ended up getting screwed. Every time!

By this time, I was on the edge of the bench and said, "Oh, what the hell!" So, I started walking toward the commotion. I was in no hurry, mind you; I was just walking at a leisurely pace. As the lady started screaming, I kind of picked up speed. When I reached the shrubbery, I saw this guy on top of her pulling down her shorts. Her shorts were down around her knees, so I screamed at the guy, saying, "Hey, what you doing there? Let her go." He turned around and looked at me and told me to mind my own business and to go fuck myself.

Oh, hell no. He didn't just tell me that. I jumped into the bushes, then on top of his ass, and started swinging at him. I must say, I was putting some nice licks upside his head and eventually, I was getting the best of him. The next thing I knew, the lady was on the top of my back, hitting me upside the head with her shoe.

"What the fuck is going on?" I said. Now, I was fighting the two of them. Hey, I ain't no fool, the first chance I got, I got the hell out of there. I made it to a bunch of trees, dropped to the ground breathing hard, and looked back. There was the lady helping the guy off the ground and giving him a big hug, cleaning his face and crying. After that, they both left the area arm in arm. Now, tell me if life ain't a bitch.

I'm getting my ass beat more outside of prison then inside. Maybe somebody's trying to tell me something? Maybe I should stay right where I am and be happy with that. One morning, before breakfast and right after I got in, I heard some commotion down the cellblock. They had guards running from all over, it seemed as though one of the inmates had hung himself. I found out it was in cell #101—a kid who had only been in solitary for 3 to 4 months. When he first came in a gangbanger, and mad at the world, he said he could take anything the prison had to throw at him. For the first two months, he was giving the guards all kinds of hell. He kind of reminded me of the way I was. Then, after a while, it started tapering off. Around the fourth month, he started asking to be released and around the fifth month, he started begging to be released. Some people just can't take solitary. Who am I kidding? A lot of people can't handle solitary. Occasionally, officer Rogers would pass by my cell and would mention the inmate in cell number 101 and toward the end, he would say he wasn't going to make it. A few days after, the kid hung himself. Officer Rogers passed by my cell and said. "See, I told you. He only lasted 150 days out of 180. Won me 100 clams off that one." You see, we know the guards would place bets on how long an inmate would make it before he totally broke down. If he was originally given 6 months, he could possibly get out in 3 or 4 months, depending on his behavior. Some guys had been in the hole for years and they had to be some strong-minded individuals, or they just like being alone. I think they still have bets on me, even though I've been here way pass my two-year time.

Six months later, I came up for review again, and this time, I was shackled. They put chains around my waist and handcuffs on my wrist. I also had a chain going down to the cuffs that were around my ankles, and this was hooked to the floor. I must say, they had me pretty much locked down, and taking no chances. This time, the committee consisted of all males and by looking at them, I could tell they had been around the Cabbage Patch.

"Good morning, John," one of them said. "Doing well and having a nice day, I hope?"

All I did was look at him. After all, what was I supposed to say?

"Let's see, John," he said. "It's been six months since that last incident you had, and we hear you had no write ups since then and your attitude has change considerably. I see you have another six months to go in the hole if all goes well, and another two years before your release from prison. We could release you from the hole right now, with time served if we wanted to and if I had a good breakfast this morning, and if my wife gave me sex last night, and if I was getting a raise in pay. But since I'm not getting any of those things, you're not getting out of the hole," he said. "Is there anything you'd like to say before you return to your cell?"

"No, sir," I said. "I appreciate the time you and these other two assholes took to deny my return to the population. I hope you all rot in hell. Thank you, sir!" I had to say something to them or it just wouldn't have been me.

One night, I got this idea to go into the committee room and check my records. I figured what, and I'll have half the night to do it. The guards don't check that place and no one gets there until 6 a.m. Plus, I could make myself some coffee before I leave. I doubt if the members all come in together, and whoever heard of someone saying, "Who made the coffee?" at 6 in the morning? No one gives a damn. They just want the coffee to be made.

The next morning, I was there in the office. It looked different with the lights off and no guards, and no committee members sitting behind the desk. And best of all, it felt good not to be chained to the chair.

I walked around, and I even sat in the members' chair and put my feet up on the desk. I walked over to the computer and hit the enter button. What luck, no password installed? Well, it is a prison and I guess they trust each other. That's shit I know. These guard have locks on everything, maybe some for the inmates but a lot from each other. I don't think it would have mattered anyway about the password, Centrale would have gotten around that anyway.

The first thing I did was bypass the main prison and went straight for the hole personnel. 158 inmates to date, minus the one in cell number 101 who committed suicide a few days before. That cell is still empty but due to be occupied soon—they never stay empty for long. The inmate in cell #132 went from 6 months to indefinite. He was a serial killer named Wilson. There were three inmates like Wilson who have been locked up for over 20 years. That makes my little two to three years seem like a piece of cake. The first thing I did was look up my records. As you would have guessed, they had me from the time I entered the prison up until that last review.

Of course, they had about 25 pages of material on me, especially when I went berserk almost a year ago now. They even had me pulling the clothes off one of the judges, everything short of molesting her. If it wasn't for the video, they would have gotten me for that too. My records show I had close to 180 days before I come up for review again. I changed that to 165 days. Oh, what the hell? Why not 145 days? If they catch it, they can blame it on computer error or human error. I was about to shut down the unit when I decided to check some of the other guys' time, starting with cell number 1.

I did the same thing with theirs as I did with my own—giving some a little less time. The serial killers, psychopaths and people like that, who had no chance of ever getting out, I left them alone. I checked the clock and noticed it was 4:35. One thing I had forgotten about working on a computer was that it will snatch the time right away from you without you knowing it. I located the coffee pot and grounds and made a pot of coffee. I always could make a decent cup of coffee. So, I helped myself to a cup. Why not? I made it.

The first person that opened the office door was the secretary and the first thing she smelled was the coffee. She assumed one of the guards had come in a little early and made the coffee. She walked over and poured herself a cup. As a coffee lover, she approved after her first sip. Whoever the coffee maker was, she must complement him, or her. As the rest of the group came in and had their coffee, they all commented on it and wondered who made it. But, no one ever owned up to it.

Most inmates keep up with their time, some better than the office, so when several them started to get released early they wondered why, but never said anything to the guards. Inmates know how to keep their mouths shut; it's part of the prison law.

One of the inmates went into the office for his 6 month review, and an officer referred to him leaving before he thought he was eligible but then he asked the secretary and she said, "It's right here on the computer. It says there's nothing wrong. You have that printout in your hand, so if you like to call the front office and asked for verification, you can."

"No, no. I wasn't trying to question your word but just questioning your figures. Just disregard what I said." The inmate just smiled at the encounter between the two and dropped his head.

Officer Rankins wasn't having it. He knew something was wrong, he just couldn't put his finger on it. Too many inmates seem to be getting released before their time. Now, he knew men got released all the time but not this many, and not this often. "If the secretary would help instead of thinking she knows everything, I believe I could figure it out. And if the old girl hadn't been here so long, giving her tenure around here, plus weight that no old person should have. And the main office people just love her to death. The computer is never wrong, and I'm gonna prove it.

She needs to retire, like, five years ago." Rankins made pretexts that he had some work to do, so he stayed over after everyone else left. He walked over to the computer and began his investigation. For about the first 2 hours, nothing popped up at him, but then he started putting little findings together. He decided to start at cell #1 of 158. At #6, he noticed the guy just got released a couple of days ago, on April 17, when he was due to be released on June 2. That was 49 days before he was due to be released. Now, how in the hell did that happen? He found the same thing with 15 other inmates. "Mrs. Series, the secretary, said everything she has on the computer comes from the main office, and I'm looking at the computer now. The printouts all come from the main office. I'm thinking someone is screwing around with the records. Either here in this office, or in the main office. Now, if I can prove that, the main office will be my next stop, but it won't be as easy to go through their records. And if we find an inside person doing this, that's going to be something else. If I can prove that, I could be in for a promotion, and maybe get out of this hellhole. The inmates aren't the only ones who hate this place. The first chance I get, I'm out of here. I should talk to Mrs. Series about this first, but I already know how she feels, and if I go straight to the main office, they're going to ask me if I went through the secretary first anyway. Doing this may end up backfiring on me. Five years ago, a similar situation happened with an older officer who tried to tell Mrs. Series how to do her job, and he ended up being forced to retire. No, I think I'd better have everything down pat before I start anything and have my own set of records."

Rankins didn't leave the office and the prison until 11:30 p.m. The next morning, John heard Officer Rogers and another officer talking.

"I hear Rankins didn't leave the office till 11:30 last night? Is he pushing for a promotion or something?" Officer Rogers said.

"I don't know," the other said, "but he's caught wind of something and somebody's about to get fucked. I hear he and the secretary got into it the other day about the time the men were getting or not getting, and she tore into him. You know, he's one of those guys that holds a grudge. He'll get back at you, even if it is a woman. He better have his shit together," Roger said. "Mrs. Series is a tough old bitty. A couple of employees have left here because of her, and not of their own free choice."

"Well, what you know about that, they're fighting between themselves about that stunt I pulled."

"Now, this could be fun! Maybe I could give Rankins just enough rope to hang himself."

Part 4

"What do you want Irma? For me to come here every night? If I do that, you'll be tired of me before I get out of prison. I don't want to wear out my welcome."

"You could never do that, John. Besides, you got somewhere else to be? And you're right, I would like to see you every night. You know we don't have to screw every time you come, we could just talk. I could fix you a nice dinner and we could just sit here and talk."

"You've been doing all that already, and I really appreciate that, but you know what I really want is a pizza. A large pizza with pepperoni, sausage, mushrooms and peppers—the works."

"If that's all you want, John, there's a pizza place that's open all night. I'll call," she said.

"How long will it take?" I said.

"About 45 minutes," she said.

"There's no need wasting that much time waiting for a pizza. Do you have any of that vodka left? And sex right now wouldn't be out of the question."

"John, I don't think you know what you want," she said.

Maybe not, I thought to myself, but I know how to get off that subject.

"After sex and pizza," Irma said to John. "Do you just come here to visit me on these trips, or do you go other places?"

John thought about that question for about a second, then decided to come clean. After all, she had been straight with me so why not do the same? So, I said, "The only place I go is here to see you; there is nowhere else I would want to go. Why do you ask?"

"I was just thinking," she said, "maybe I could take one of those trips with you, it would be fun. If we went to a place like Jamaica, since you have to leave at five in the morning, I could just stay there until you came back for me the next night.

Maybe I could even stay two or three nights, now wouldn't that be something?"

"You know," John said, "I never thought of that. I'd have to bring it up to Centrale. You know, he's funny about that kind of thing. I asked him once about getting me out of prison permanently but he told me his people wouldn't approve. They have some weird philosophy about right and wrong, and paying your debts. So, like I said, I don't know, but I'll ask him."

"How long do you have to go on your sentence, John? You should be ready to get out about now."

"Six months, 18 days. That is if they don't tack any more time on me for fucking up."

"You haven't done anything lately to get you more time, have you? After all, the life you're living now is just like you being on the outside."

"Well, I'm not on the outside, even if I do get a few hours out each night. Then, I have to eat that bad food at least twice a day, and smell that place, and listen to that loud ass noise every day.

The guards are all low life's and always fucking with me."

"That Officer Hastings, is he still giving you trouble?" Irma asked.

"Yes and no. I'm still trying to figure out how to bust his ass. If he figured out that I manipulated the computer, that will add more time to my sentence really quick."

"What are you going to do," Irma asked.

"I have to figure out some way to get rid of him and I've been thinking, I may have an ally—Mrs. Series!"

"**Officer** Rankins, I can appreciate your concern about what's going on in your section about the inmates, but Mrs. Series is doing a great job of taking care of that, and you should have talked to her first. It would have saved a lot of time and I'm sure she would have appreciated it. We think Mrs. Series is doing a great job and I'm sure if there were any problems like you say there are, Mrs.

Series would have caught them. But, to set your mind at ease, I'll have her look at your figures again and report back to me. Is that okay with you?" Mr. Ramose said. Mr. Ramose was the Warden of the prison and in charge of everyone and everything in and around the yard. He had the final say. After thinking about it, Rankins thought he would do the right thing and go to the Warden, tell him his suspicions, and hope he'd understand. However, I see he didn't. He didn't even give me a chance to explain it to him. It seems like Mrs. Series explained to him what my concerns were "at lunch". She assured him there was nothing to it. See what happens when you try to do the right thing? Now what? That fool wouldn't even look at the paperwork I had. I'm sure I'll hear Mrs. Series mouth when I get back. I want hear the last of this! The hell with that; I'm still not giving up.

A few days later, John heard that Rankins had gotten his ass eaten out by the warden and then to top that off, Mrs. Series had a turn at him in front of everyone in the office. They said she had no class doing something like that but she did things like that all the time, so what's the big deal? She did it to the right guy! Just when you thought you had seen it all, Rankins started doing things that no one suspected he would. Whenever the future inmates came up for intake, he would find some reason to add more time to their sentence and push the other two committee members to agree with him. He later told one that that's what they deserve anyway. "By the time I'm through, they'll have double their time." Mrs. Series mentioned to him that what he was doing was wrong, but Rankins told her she had told him to stay out of her business, so he would like the courtesy of her doing the same. Warden Ramose had left for an out of country tour to visit other prisons, so she couldn't report what she knew Rankins was doing. She knew that sometimes, Warden Ramose would check on his e-mail from wherever he was, so she decided to e-mail him.

Rankins got wind of this and decided to delete the message at the receiving end, which meant breaking into the main office—Warden Ramone's office. Desperate times call for desperate measures, he thought.

Rumors went around. even in the hole I only got out an hour a day in the yard, sometimes there's a guy on the left and right of me and I would converse with them. You could make eye contact with the guys in the building and then use sign language. Then, there are always the guards talking and the kites—the notes—flying around. There's always something.

A few days later, Rankins stayed over again. He said he had some work to catch up on. The computer still didn't have a password but Mrs. Series had one on a private program, but he didn't know it. "If Warden Ramose has a password on his computer, I'm screwed. If that's the case, I'm doing all of this for nothing."

Two days later, and a week before the warden returned, Rankins was in his office and on his computer. Rankins got to the e-mail section and found there was no password for his mail. There were three e-mail notices from Mrs. Series and one of them was the one he was after. It contained two pages of the bullshit she thought he had done wrong, and in her opinion, she felt he should be terminated. "That bitch!" he said and deleted the letter! A week later, the warden returned and the next day, called Rankins to his office.

"Officer Rankins, before you say anything, tell me this. What were you doing in my office?"

"Sir, I was never in your office; you must be mistaken."

"So, you deny ever being in my office?"

"Yes, sir," Rankin said.

"Maybe you can explain this," he said as he opened the top drawer of his desk and took out on object, laid it out on the desk and slid it over to him. On the desk was a money clip with the name officer Rankins 2001, for his 10 years' service. Rankins just looked at it and asked Warden Ramose, "Where did you find my money clip? I've been looking for that for over a week.

"Do you have any idea where you might have lost it?" the warden asked.

"No, sir. I have no idea at all," Rankins said.

"I found it underneath my desk," Ramose said. "Now, what would your money clip be doing underneath my desk? I'll tell you what, Officer Rankins. Don't say anything; just listen. I came back to the office and the first thing I do is check my e-mail, and guess what? One of my messages is missing. Now, how do I know this? You see, all my e-mail that comes to my office, a copy also goes to my home. Officer Rankins, I always read my home messages just in case I miss something, and I sure missed something this time. Would you happen to know what that was, Officer Rankins? The message Mrs. Series sent me here in the office, it's not here. But it is at my home. That tells me someone deleted the one in the office. I've spoken to Mrs. Series, so I know the message in question. Officer Rankins, I think it would be best if you turn in your resignation."

John was being taken to the yard a few days later and the inmate in the section next to him mentioned that Officer Rankins was resigning. "They say he left crying like a baby. Before he left, he blamed Mrs. Series for everything. It looks like he was going to go upside her head but they stopped him."

Well, what do you know about that? Finding that money clip with his name on it and putting it into the Warden's office where he could find it was a nice touch. It worked out better than I had expected. Next!

I spoke to Centrale about taking Irma on a few of the trips with me and he said it wouldn't be a problem. To surprise her, the first trip I wanted to take her on was to Montego Bay, Jamaica. We lay on the beach and drank rum and coke. Irma always looked good in a bikini, and everything she had was in season, just right for the picking. She swam and walked up and down the beach and I just watched her. We made love on the beach under the stars, listened to Jamaican music under the moon, and no one seemed to care because everyone else was doing the same thing. After all, this was Jamaica.

We had decided she would stay there while I went back and meet up with her that night. That worked out great, and we did that for a week. Acapulco, Mexico was next. Then, Argentina, Hawaii, Cuba, Australia, Hong Kong, Berlin and Amsterdam. We made love in every one of those places, and before we knew it, my time with the state was over and they were calling me into the committee room to talk about my release.

"John," one said. "You about ready to get out of here?"

"Yes, sir," I said.

"You've been in here for how long now?" he asked.

"18 months, and 3 weeks," I said.

"You know, John, you should have been out of here a year and a half ago if not for you acting up."

"Yes, sir, I know," I said.

"You won't even have to go to population; straight on out the door. Well, another two weeks and you'll be home free. I must say, John, it's been as though you haven't even been here at all the last eight months. How did you do it?"

"I just learned my lesson, sir, and decided if I wanted to get out of here, I'd better straighten up."

"And you did, John. You did. How does November 13th sound to you? That'll be not quite two weeks from now."

"I'll tell you what, sir. I could leave tomorrow if you need the space." All the committee members, guards, and even Mrs. Series got a little chuckle out of that one.

"Two weeks, John, and you'll be out of here."

That following night, Irma and I went back to where it all began: Jamaica. We spent a week there, just in case it would be our last. That last week, I knew the officers were going to keep a close eye on me, plus they wanted me to get the hell out of there too. That was cool. I was ready to go.

"John, this has really been nice," Irma said. "But this isn't real and I am ready for some normalcy. You know what I mean?" I did and she did, so all I could say was, "Set me free."

I told Centrale I was getting out and he was happy for me. He said he would be going to another galaxy soon and said I should think about going with him—it would be the chance of a lifetime.

Now, how about that? If I could do all the things Centrale could do, I'd never have to worry about anything the rest of my days. Sure, I'd go. I didn't even need to think about that.

"One thing, John. Once I leave, and if you decide not to go, you won't be able to contact me again."

Irma! What about Irma? I don't think that would be the place for her, she's not ready for the stars, and she's not ready for another galaxy far, far away. She can stay right here. I'm getting tired of her anyway.

When the day came to leave, I did the reverse of what I did coming in here: I took my jail clothes off, got searched again, and went to the holding cell and put on my civilian clothes. I picked up the little trinkets I came in with, like my wallet with pictures, $35 cash and $.26 in change. I also got $50 from the good state of Ohio for being their guest and lots of advice from a few of the staff.

"Don't come back."

John was almost out the last gate when it happened. The guard made a sly remark and it happened to be Officer Rogers, reassigned from the hole. He had been talking shit to him for almost three years. John could see Irma across the street waiting for him and waving. She was waiting to drive him home. He looked at the guard who was smiling, and who said, "You'll be back; they always come back." Then, it happened; something just snapped in him and all reason left him. Nothing mattered, his mind went blank, and that's when he hit him. He felt the blow from his fingertips to the top of his back molar. He had never hit a man that hard in his life before. He could see the guard's eyes roll back in his head before he hit the floor. John never saw a person out cold with his eyes open. "I never left," John said to Officer Rogers, although Officer Rogers couldn't hear him. The other officers grabbed John, took his bag and re-shackled him.

"You'll do a year in the hole for this, John," one of the guards said. The last thing John saw was Irma getting into her car and driving away; she didn't look back.

2

Way to heaven!   Part 1

I waited until he opened his door and walked in his house. I would give him 10 minutes, then I would walk up to his door, ring his bell and when he opened it, I'd put one 22 hollow point right between his eyes. It was 10:30 p.m., and the street was quiet and lined with high dollar houses, with hardly any traffic at all. I was told he lived alone, so there will be no witnesses. This should be a piece of cake.

Two weeks ago, I was called to handle a job that was in my profession. I kill people—for a price, that is. I've been in this business for 10 years now and I'm good at it, if I don't say so myself. I'll go anywhere for a dollar. I'm kind of like that old Western "have gun will travel" I like that old movie! And it says a lot about me. The call I received was from a voice that I imagined was the same I've been hearing for years and may have been from another country for all I know. Nevertheless, it was the same voice. So, this person had been around for as long as I have. He says just enough, and he's off the line. The envelope will be at the bus station, and the locker number is 246. It will have all my instructions in it. The pay will be the same as always—they always seem to know my price, all depending on the hit. No complaints so far. I picked up the package and returned to my apartment, placed it on my coffee table, walked over to my bar and poured a glass of Johnny Walker red scotch over ice. I took off my dress coat and sat on the couch, put my feet up on the table and grabbed the envelope. I pulled out the contents and sat back to see what I had. A 7 x 5 color photo of a white male, with his bio on the back. He was 52 years old, had salt and pepper hair with a receding hairline, brown eyes and a Hitler mustache. He wore round book keeper reading glasses, and there was a small half-inch scar on his right cheek. Aside from the photo, his address in Phoenix Arizona was also included, along with my pay of $20,000. No mention of family or why he needed to be killed. There was nothing like that, but it wasn't my business anyway. However, there was a post-script that said the contract was to be completed in two weeks. Once I finish the hit, there would be another 20-grand waiting for me.

Joseph Bishop was a 39-year-old Italian American. He was 5 feet 10, with black hair and eyes. He had no facial hair but had a small scar on the tip of his nose. He always wore a black suit, hat and a red and white bowtie. He had a small tattoo of a heart on the back of his left hand. Joseph had a high-pitched voice like it was coming out of his nose passage. Killing was a business to him and he didn't look at it any other way. He only killed who he was hired to kill and that's all. Okay, occasionally, there was collateral damage, but that's to be expected.

The train from Chicago to Phoenix Arizona took 18 hours. He could have gotten there sooner if he had flown but he wasn't a fan of flying. If God would have meant for man to fly, he would have given them wings.

Once in Phoenix, he had to take off his wool suit and get into something lighter—all black, of course, he even went Western. Black Western cowboy hat, black shirt and pants, and to top it off, Western boots. He fit right in!

The difference in the weather was a considerable 30°. Well, what could he expect, this was the desert? Once he got off the train, it felt like a sauna. He immediately ran to the hotel and took a shower.

I parked in the driveway and walked up the steps to the front door. I had the Beretta in hand with the silencer attached. I didn't even have the weapon down at my side because I knew he was home alone and would be the only one who would open the door, and then I'd pop him. But it didn't turn out like that. It didn't turn out like that at all! instead, a 12-year-old little girl opened the door and the moment I saw her, I had shot her. The surprise that registered on her face was no less surprising, then what was on mine.

She just dropped to the floor where she stood with the hole between her eyes. I just stood there and watched her fall. That's when I noticed "him", my target, coming out of the kitchen. He saw the girl on the floor and started running toward her. Before he had gotten 10 feet, I had shot him three times. I went over to him and shot him once more in the head. As I was walking out the door, I glanced down at the girl, shook my head and said, "Wrong place, wrong time!"

A week later, in Chicago, I received a phone call. "Joseph," it was the voice. "I wanted to let you know that we're not too happy with the last job you did. It was very sloppy, and we hope it will be the last one of those."

"I understand," I said. "But those things happen. You have some good days and some bad," I said.

"In our business." the voice said, "it shouldn't be like that. We can't afford that. I was told to tell you that with the amount we are paying you, we expect better service."

"I hear you," Joseph said.

Joseph didn't normally do this but he decided to look up his last target's background. So, he went down to the city library to retrieve the Phoenix Arizona city newspaper and looked for the date of the hit.

The Phoenix Times, November 18, 1952
Murder by 2... The headlines said.

At approximately 11 p.m., a Mr. Robert Morris and a young female were both murdered in their home. Morris had just gotten back from a meeting at the CDR building where he was the chairman. He had been under investigation for child molestation for the past 12 months. The young girl has not been identified yet.

Joseph located the newspaper for 3 days later.

The Phoenix Times, November 22, 1952

There are still no suspects for the murders of Mr. Robert Morris and his 12-year-old guest.

Neighbors say she is Dorothy Lange and has been staying with Morris for some time but hardly came out of the house. She has been seen swimming in the pool in the nude. Her next of kin have been notified.

I remember that little girl; I really didn't mean to kill her but things happen. So, why is it still bothering me? I tried drinking it away the last few nights but I'm still waking up in the middle of the night with cold sweats, picturing myself at the front door, the door opening, the little girl standing there and me shooting her. Seeing a hole in her head and she falling to the floor, with me standing over her. It's all happening, like in slow motion. It shouldn't bother me. After all, I've been in this business for years now, but never killed a kid.

Maybe it'll go away. This is not good for my kind of work.

Part 2

A month later, the call came—that voice again. He informed me that another package would be at the train station, in locker number 742. I picked the package up, took it to my apartment and emptied the contents. There was a 7 x 5 photo of a young lady, around 28 years of age. She was a redhead with green eyes, and was 5 foot 4 1/2, and one hundred and 50 pounds. Her name was Nora Pines. Her address was in Rome, New York. The postscript read that the job was to be completed within the week—nothing fancy, just get it done.

Rome, New York from Chicago should have taken less than two days—a day or two to get settled and find my way around. A week should do it!

The package also included $20,000—my usual fee. I didn't consider the cold and how much snow upstate New York had in January. It took me a day and a half to reach my destination, then it was hell trying to get around the place, even though it was a small town. Nora stayed in the lower part of town—you could say the red-light district. The duplex she lived in was kept up nice, but you could tell they were fighting a losing battle. The street was blocked in with snow where only one car could get by at a time. The sidewalks were not passable, and there was no place to park.

I found a parking spot two blocks away where the snowplow had passed through. I walked back to Nora's House and knocked on the door. I had the Beretta and the silencer both ready—both underneath the package I held in my hand. When the door opened and Nora Pines appeared in front of me, my mouth opened and I was stunned.

"Yes?" she said. "Can I help you?" When the surprise passed and my head cleared, I shot her right between the eyes, then I walked away. I went back to my rental car, then to my hotel room. The next day, I was on my way back to Chicago. All I thought about was Nora Pines. Back at my apartment, I took a shower and lay on my bed with my hands behind my head and thought about Nora Pines.

Nora Pines looked just like Dorothy Lange, the little girl from Arizona, right down to her ponytail and the mole below her lower lip.

A few days later, I decided to treat myself and have lunch at Carlos Italian restaurant and walk along the Mag Mile—an upscale section of Chicago—to get a few outfits I've been needing. It's been a while since I had done that. Finally, I think I'll call over one of the ladies to end the night. Freda—I haven't seen her in a couple of weeks. Foxy Freda! 5 foot 8, black hair, black eyes. A midsize woman—she's got to have some beef on her. Size 12 through 18 for me, and that's Freda. The last time she brought one of her friends with her but I don't know how they do it. I have a hard time concentrating on just one. Oh, well. What the hell, it doesn't happen that often anyway. But I think for tonight, it'll just be me and Freda.

That night, and right on time at 9 p.m., Freda walked through the door—all one hundred and 75 pounds of her. She wasn't alone; she brought a friend. The best thing about having a prostitute versus a girlfriend is that the next morning, the prostitute knows when it's time to leave, while the girlfriend has her toothbrush in her bag and has already made plans for the rest of the day for you. So, when Freda and her friend got up, I ordered breakfasts, and we sat out on the patio and ate. Both were in their panties, without any bras. After eating, they got dressed and I paid them, plus a hefty tip. They earned it. Then, they left. Now, that's business.

"You'll call me?" Freda asked.

"I'll call you," I said.

I made my way back down to the library and picked up the Rome, New York, Times. This was getting to be a habit but I just had to know.

Rome New York: Front Door Murder.
In the middle of the afternoon, a 28-year-old Caucasian woman was murdered at her front door by an unknown person or persons. The murder victim's name was Nora Pines. Ms. Pines happened to be on a jury of an embezzler in city court of Judge J.D Barns. It was said that she was the only holdout for a guilty verdict. Ms. Pines was unemployed and living alone.

So, that's the story on Nora. My bet is they tried to buy her off and either it wasn't enough, or they just wanted this guy to go down and she wouldn't play along. They have people like that in the world—honest people! Normally, the people that employ me pay for guys to get off; not to go down. If they did that, then there is something in it for them. This sounds like a scapegoat to me and Nora Pains got caught in the middle.

The dreams never stop; they didn't come every night but most nights. I knew something was wrong when I went onto the next hit. This time, it was McAllen, Texas, which borders Mexico right on the river.

I found out later that two elderly sisters didn't want to sell their 10-acre ranch and for reasons of their own, the people I worked for wanted it. The only people in the house were supposed to be the two sisters. The granddaughter was off at school. She would inherit the place and would then sell the place after the sisters were gone. I was told to kill both sisters. McAllen was one hundred and ten degrees in the shade. I rented a Jeep and headed for the ranch. It took a while to find the place but eventually, I located it at around 11 a.m. It was even hot at that time of day. On seeing the place, it didn't look worth killing two old ladies over. But there I go again, trying to figure out the reason why. Why this, why that, instead of just doing my job.

I drove into the yard and the first person I saw was one of the sisters feeding the chickens and calling to them, saying, "Here chick, here chick, chick chick chick." This was going to be a piece of cake, and I didn't think about it anymore. I took out the Beretta without the silencer and walked over to her. She stood up to greet me and saw the Beretta in my hand. She dropped the pan she had in her hands to feed the chickens with and started to run. She called for Sarah—I assumed she was calling for her sister. I shot her three times in the back, walked up to her, and shot her again in the head.

I walked past her and on toward the house. Within 20 feet of the door, I saw Sarah coming out. In stride, I lifted the Beretta, pointed it at her, and shot her twice in the chest. She fell back into the kitchen. I walked up to her and shot her once more in the head. Old people shouldn't suffer! I walked through the house to make sure no one else was around. If there was, I'd have to deal with them too. I noticed they still had a few slices of bacon and a biscuit or two, plus orange juice on the table, so I helped myself. As I was eating, I noticed pictures on the wall and I stood up to take a closer look.

One was of the two sisters alone, another was a sister and some man, and another was the two sisters and one man. There was one with a lady and a baby on the river, and the lady Then, I spotted a picture that made me stop in my tracks. I stopped chewing the bacon, and the glass I was holding was spilling over. No, it can't be. The picture I saw was of a teenager of about 14 or 15, and I be damned if she didn't look like the girl from Arizona and New York. I backed up from the picture, dropped the glass and ran out the house.

Chicago in the spring is a very good time to take a stroll and give thanks and reminisce. Lakeshore Drive is miles of beautiful scenery and even if you've seen it before, it's like you're seeing it again for the very first time. There is no place like Chicago! I'd rather live here than anywhere else in the world. I've had work here but just like anything else, you go where the work is. I'm glad to say there hasn't been that much work in Chicago—for me that is.

Why am I having these problems? I don't know. Maybe I need to see a psychiatrist. The dreams and pictures I've been seeing of Dorothy are beyond my understanding.

Forty-five minutes into my walk, I passed St. Luke's Catholic Church. I stopped outside and just stood there for a few minutes. I decided to walk in—it couldn't hurt. Walking the 30 steps that led to the doors of the chapel was something I hadn't done since I was a boy. I don't even remember what I'm supposed to do when I walk through the door—put water on my head and kneel or something. Maybe give some money? I know there's a place to drop off a little change somewhere—there always is. I walked halfway down the aisle and took the second seat in and looked around. It was so quiet. It wasn't this quiet in my apartment, minus Freda that is.

The windows of the church were beautiful, and I couldn't remember who the statues were of, but little by little, my past started coming back to me.

I went on my first hit before I was baptized—it was when I was with my parents. Dad did the hit; mom drove the car and I was in the back. I was told later that the hit was a taxi driver who wouldn't turn over part of his fee to the powers that be. There're so many chances they give you, then they make an example out of somebody. You! Each Sunday, we went to church to have our sins forgiven. This way, my parents felt everything would be all right. A lot of people in my profession felt it was all right to do what they were doing if they would only confess every Sunday in church—thinking that the way to get to heaven is through confessing. When I was eight years old, I was the lookout for my parents. When I was thirteen, I graduated to my first hit and when I was sixteen, I was going solo. I've been hired out ever since. My parents had since retired from the business and had moved to Florida. It's been a long time but in other ways, it seemed like only yesterday. It's also been profitable and enlightening, and at times even enjoyable. That is, until now! My parents never told me about this part of the business. I need to overcome this; I must overcome this. I haven't been coming to mass. Maybe that has something to do with it. The confession booth was over on the left side of the chapel. Maybe if!

I walked over and went into the booth and sat down. The priests pulled the curtain aside and asked, "Yes, my son. What is your sin?" Joseph said nothing, so the priest asked again. "Yes, my son? Would you like to confess your sins?"

"Father, would you mind if I just sit here for a few minutes and not say anything?"

"It is somewhat unusual but if that's what you want, my son! Let me know when you're ready."

Ten minutes later, the priest looked into the booth and noticed that Joseph had gone. In fact, Joseph had left five minutes earlier. The priest assumed he was a troubled young man.

Joseph had gone back to the walkway and was sitting on a bench watching the water and the sun go down. The chapel just wasn't doing it for him. It was peaceful and all, but something was still missing. And he didn't have to think too hard before he saw all three girls. He felt he was losing it. What could be happening to him?

Dad! Maybe I'll call dad. He's always got advice; I may not like it but he's always got advice.

"Well, it's been a while since we heard from you, Joseph," his dad said to him. "Your mother isn't here right now; she went to town to get her hair done."

"That's okay, Dad. I wanted to talk to you anyway."

"Well, all right, Joe. What about?"

"It's about the job. I know we don't talk about that on the phone but there is really something that's bothering me."

"For you to call me and ask me about whatever, it must be important," he said.

"It is, Dad. Now, you're going to have to stay with me on this, are you ready?"

"Yeah, I'm ready, go."

"There was this job I went on and took care of it the best I could, but there was someone else there and they got caught in the mix. A kid! The next job I went on, those people looked like the last. And I haven't been able to get them out of my mind."

"That's not good, Joseph," his dad said.

"That's not good at all," Joseph said. "There was a third job and I ran into almost the same situation, except this time, it was a picture I saw, and it looked just like the other two. Now, I'm having nightmares and cold sweats once or twice a week."

"Have you been going to mass, Joseph? You always been taught to go to mass and go to confession. Tell the priest everything; it'll cleanse your soul. I told you that years ago, and it works."

"I went to confession but I didn't speak to the priest, I just sat there and then I walked out."

"Well, next time, talk to him. Place all those problems on his shoulders—that's what he's there

for. Is that all you need? My golfing buddies are
here."

"That's it, Dad. Thanks!"

Before he hung up, he told me to go to
confession. I should have known that's what he
would say—mass settles everything for him. I'm
not too keen on telling anyone all my business; I
don't care who they are. Maybe I could just go
there and sit around for an hour or so, and throw a
few coins in the collection box—that should work.

Two weeks later, I was sitting in the same spot
in the chapel when the priest came by.

"Hello," he said. "I see you're back. Are you
going to stop by and see me today?"

"Stop by," I said. I acted like I didn't know
what he was talking about.

"The confession booth," he said.

"I am, father, but not today. I'm just not ready
today. Besides, I'm about to leave town for
Louisiana. I should be back in a week or so."

"Like I said before, my son, whenever you're ready."

Part 3

Two days later, I was on a train headed for Toronto, Canada. I wasn't about to tell the good priest where I was really going; I never have!

This time, it was a hit on a municipal judge on vacation with his mistress. This one had to look like an accident, and this time, I had help—the mistress! Damn if I knew how she got involved in this, but there it was. I've never worked with anyone before and they know that. Very few people have ever seen me, and there is a reason for that. For one thing, that's the way my parents taught me, and another is if you fuck up, you have no one to blame but yourself. But, since they're paying the bills and have been for as long as I've been around, I guess it'll be okay.

The judge was an outdoorsy person, so they'll be doing a lot of camping and stuff. An accident should be easy.

Judge Stephen B. Boyd was 48 years old, 5 feet 11 and 210 pounds. He had a full head of gray and black hair, a full mustache and was very fit. He was an avid outdoorsy man and runner. He has been married for 12 years and has two kids—an eight-year-old girl, and an eleven-year-old boy. Judge Boyd is one of the youngest judges on the bench and is expected to advance to the state Supreme Court within the next five years. There's just one flaw the judge has—he loves the ladies. If it wasn't for his judgeship, he would get divorced and marry his mistress. However, the way it is now, if he wants to stay a judge and make it to the state court, he should stay married. Unfortunately, his mistress doesn't see it that way, and feels if she can't have him, no one else will. But, the judge wants both women. The trip to

Canada was to try and convince her to hang in there. The cabin he had rented was one of 8, which was set in the hills right above the little village in an area for hikers, joggers, bikers and mountain climbers. It was a one-bedroom cabin with a family room and fireplace, a kitchen and bath. The cabins were not close together—they were mostly spread out, and there wasn't even a way to drive up to it—you had to walk. But he knew all that before he rented the place. This wasn't a problem for an outdoorsy man, and it didn't bother Pearl—his lover—because that's how they got together, with her being an outdoorsy person just like him.

After unloading their stuff, Stephen told Pearl he was going for a run, but she didn't join him. Stephen walked out the door and around the cabin and up the hill. There were still an hour and a half of light left. Joseph was coming down the hill and passed the judge as he was going up. He knew the cabin the judge was in, and he had rented his own a day before the judge arrived. They were going to be there for a week, so he had time to come up with a plan. He needed to talk to the girl—that was his next move. I'll leave it up to her, maybe she has some ideas.

I passed by their cabin and saw the girl at the front door. She saw me but of course, she didn't know who I was. I guess we'll have to meet sooner rather than later. She was a fine-looking woman! She stood at 5 foot 5 or 6, and one hundred and 35 pounds. She had red hair, which was cut in a bob. She was wearing shorts—climbing shorts I guess you'd call them—and a halter. Nice legs!

She reminded me of an old girlfriend of mine. I have to laugh every time I think of her. We'd be out in my ride in the boondocks and I was trying to get a little bit. She'd get out the car and I'd get out right behind her. She'd start running around the car and I'd be right behind her, like we were on a race track or something. Three times around the car and eventually, she would make it to the back door, open it and jump in, and we'd bang for hours. Every time! I never could understand that, but what did I care? As long as I got the drawls. Those were the days!

The next morning, after breakfast, Pearl and Judge Boyd went for their morning jog. Two hours later, they were back in the cabin. Shower, sex and a nap.

Just before lunch, they found that they had no bread, so Pearl volunteered to go to the village and pick up a loaf. On the way, she made a slight detour to the lookout point and there she met Joseph. The voice had told her what kind of car he'd be driving and what he looked like. She left her car and went over to his.

"Joseph?" she asked.

"Yes," he said. "Before we start, I want to tell you straight out that I didn't approve of this assignment, I usually work alone."

"So, I've been told, Joseph, but you will do what you are hired to do, won't you?"

"I will! How do you want to do this?"

"You've been up the mountain and around the trail, haven't you? Well, there is a spot about three miles up that has the perfect location for him to go over. You were told it needs to look like an accident?"

"Yes, I've been told that, but wouldn't they focus on you when something happens to him?" Joseph said.

"It doesn't matter, and I want his wife to know that I was the last one with him when he died."

"They may try to blame you for his death even though it looks like an accident. Are you ready for that? After all, he is a judge."

"I've considered all that and I'm willing to take the risk," Pearl said.

"Okay, when do you want to do this and how" Joseph asked.

"Maybe Thursday, that morning. I'll be running in front of him and I'll stumble. He will stop and try to help me. You'll be coming down the mountain—at that spot, it's a 50-foot drop. As you stop to help, you push him over. Simple!"

"Yeah, simple. Sounds like it, but nothing ever goes as planned. Let me go over it in my mind. If I like it, we'll go with it."

"When will you know?" she asked.

"Let me see. We are Monday, so you will know by tomorrow, through the voice."

Later that afternoon, Joseph was in the village and passed by a chapel and decided to stop in. Wouldn't hurt. This chapel was a lot smaller than the one in Chicago, and was quainter than the other one. Big cities are like that—just overwhelming. Although the windows were there, there weren't as many. The statues were there, but they weren't as grand. There was one thing here that wasn't at the one in Chicago—that homely feeling; the feeling you get when you know you just arrived home. The feeling you get when you go to buy a new car and you know you found the right one, or the house you found after looking at 20 or more, and saying to yourself that this is the one.

I sat down in the pew and took a deep breath. I thought to myself, "home at last." I must have sat there for thirty minutes before I noticed the confession booth over in the corner near the rear of the chapel. I thought about going over and confessing my sins, remembering what Dad had advised me to do. "Hedge your bets," he said. Maybe not in those words, but same idea. I'm still having those dreams, so this could be the place to unload my troubles, as Dad put it.

In the booth, the curtain came back and the father said, "Yes, my son?"

"Forgive me, father, for I have sinned."

Joseph went on to tell him of the three girls he had recently killed and how they all resembled each other, and the nightmares he was having. He also told him of the upcoming hit on the judge and the help from the mistress. After confessing all this, Joseph walked out of the chapel feeling good. "Got that monkey off my back. Dad was right, confessing does cleanse your soul."

He was on the mountain at least 45 minutes before the judge and Pearl, and was in a good spot to watch them. The spot where the judge was to go over was two thirds the way to the top. At one and a half, Joseph started down the mountain. Two thirds of the way up, Pearl stumbled and fell, and the judge dropped to his knees beside her in concern. Joseph came into view around the bend and saw them. Pearl was on one knee and holding the other. Joseph was alongside of them and asked if he could help. The judge looked up and said, "No, thanks. It's not that bad."

When the judge turned his attention back to Pearl, that's when Joseph made his move. He lunged at the judge to push him over the edge, but the judge unexpectedly turned toward Joseph and grabbed his wrist and jerked him toward and over the cliff. Joseph screamed all the way down—all 50 feet.

Four police officers came running, huffing and puffing up the mountain. Two in uniform and two in plain clothes.

"Goddamn, judge. We thought that was you going over the edge. Sorry we couldn't get to you any sooner," said the lead detective.

"That's okay, detective. Things worked out for the best."

"Oh, Stephen. I was so afraid for you. He almost pushed you off the cliff. I'm so glad you're all right." The judge just looked at her and shook his head. "Yes," he said. "So am I!"

The next day at the station

"What are you going to do about the girl, judge?" the detective asked. "She was part of the hit too."

"Nothing," the judge said. "There is no proof and we can't prove she had any part in it. All we know is that an 'unknown guy' tried to push me off the cliff for no reason. You can't go to court with just that."

"What about your witness, judge?" the detective asked.

"Forget about the witness, detective. I think I'll just do the right thing and go back to my wife and kids. They're beginning to look better and better to me every day."

"Are you ever going to tell anyone, judge? I mean, how you found out about the hit?" the detective asked.

"That the witness was my priest and the priest is my brother? No!" he said. "It'll be our secret."

3

Love in, Love out   **Part 1**

When I first spotted the old girl, she was one of the finest girls I had ever seen. I guess I shouldn't call her on old girl, she was only 19 and I was 22, and that's just my way of speaking. It takes a little getting used to. I had been with girls just as fine but there's nothing like the latest one, she's the finest now. For some reason, you see a girl that's fine and you never think you have a chance with her, but then I found out that you never will if you don't try. I once had a girl tell me after wanting her for years when I was about to leave town that all I ever had to do was ask her. That reply from her stayed with me to this day. So, after that, I made up my mind that I was going to ask. I didn't care how many times I got shot down—and it was a lot. One girl had me at her job asking her for a date and looking like a damn fool for two hours, only to never get one. I was talking about her and I, and she was talking about her and the other guy. I learned when you out there, you have to be very humble, until you get the drawls that is. A lot of this sick stuff is just that. When I look back, I believe a lot of it was just a waste of my time. If I would have gone to somebody's school, I would have had at least a PhD for sure by now.

Instead, I got 15 minutes of nothing. One hour of getting myself together, including getting my clothes from the cleaners, getting a haircut and shave, gassing up the car and getting a car wash. You have a pint of good liquor—well, maybe the second-best liquor, and you stay up half the night, even if you don't get any drawls but just the thought of getting drawls. But don't get a player, she'll drink you under the table, frustrate you all night, and you still get no drawls. She'll say she doesn't do that on the first night, but I guess drinking all my liquor on the first date is ok. It ain't easy! Relationships are funny. You chase her, she chases him, and he chases the other woman who is most likely married. Crazy!

But, you know, I think I'm getting off track. Love, and talking about love does that to you sometime. I was beside myself. I was a young good-looking guy, so I've been told. I had a new car, two new suits and was making good money. Yeah, I couldn't go wrong. I went through all the things and "tricks" to get her to like me and get in her pants—that's all part of it. It's never easy but in the end, it's worth it. Everyone's got a game plan, including the woman. Since I never had things go my way, I diverged a plan that went like this; I told the fellows to get the word out that I didn't like this person; that I couldn't stand her. You see, I know that if you liked someone, that was all right, but they didn't have to like you back, which was cool too. They seem to like it that way, but Goddamn, don't let it be the opposite—they can't stand that. So, my strategy was this; every time I passed her, I would turn my head and walk down the street. I would always cross the street if she was coming in my direction. I noticed she would turn her head in my direction—when before she wouldn't—wondering why I had crossed the street. Eventually, she got to asking why I didn't like her. Hook, placed and set!

After that, it seemed like I couldn't get rid of her. We were like ham and cheese, Mud and Jeff, Amos and Andy. I was being loved to death. Have you ever been smothered to death with love? Always be careful what you wish for. I loved that girl and she loved me but somewhere along the way, we lost all that. I don't even think we know when or where, it wasn't like overnight but it happened gradually. That's a damn shame too because I love that feeling of being in love. Being on a high, and every time you touch the woman, you want to make love to her. You just can't keep your hands off her. It went from that to not wanting her to touch me. We no longer had any outings together, we didn't go for walks together and we had very little sex. How do you make love to a woman without touching her? Sometimes, one of us would rather be at work then at home, while the other would hate to be at home because even when you're there, it's like you're there alone—if that makes any sense. I had many loves that I thought was love but there was only one, and I miss her, and I know there'll never be another. You wonder about those couples walking down the street, hand in hand, and you say to yourself, "Are they man and wife? If so, they just got married. Or the guy that opens the door for the woman, tricks! I remember doing the same thing in the beginning, all BS! Except when I was with that special one. Everything else was totally BS. When I see these people in the park, I can just about tell who's in a relationship and who's not, and what stage of the relationship they are in. Like this guy and his girl that I saw in the park the other day. He got out of his truck and ran around to the other side and opened the door for her. Now, the girl's still sitting in the seat, mind you. So, he takes her hand and helps her out. First date, I'd bet! No doubt about it. He's trying hard, very hard. I could tell right off he was "too nice" and he will be walked on sooner than later. His proper respond should have been to get out of the truck and wait for the girl to get out, then if you want to hold hands, have at it. Some women don't want that shit. They might feel you think they are helpless or something. Which reminds me, I was at the hospital once getting ready to walk into the doctor's office. There was a lady behind me so I opened the door, stepped aside and held it for her. "Thank you," she said. "You don't see many men do that for women anymore."

Hell, no, I thought, because we don't know how women are going to act. We are damned if we do and damned if we don't. We know we are in the shit when after a few years, they start talking about us behind our backs to their friends. "He ain't this and he ain't that. I don't know what I ever saw in him." The same woman who at one point, couldn't get enough of you. "I think I just might trade his ass in." The thing she doesn't know is that one of her friends is listening to all this and she thinks the man is all right and might like to try the old boy out for herself. After all, she had said how good he was in bed at one time anyway. Better than her old man, I'd bet. There is an old saying, if you throw the trash out, there is always someone there to pick it up. Sometimes, love can be tossed out the window and you find you made a mistake and want it back, but even if you get it back, the love has gone. It'll never be like the first time, no matter how much you want it back. It'll never be the same.

For the real love, there will only be one first kiss that you'll always remember, one first feel of the breast before the kids come along and change things. And one rumble in the back seat of your first car that you'll never forget. Real love only comes around once, there are no second chances. There are just imitations after that.

It was the damnest thing. The second girl I met was the spitting image of the first. Short, 5 foot 2, one hundred and 25 pounds, with red hair. She had a pug nose and a tattoo of a deer on her left shoulder. She had an ankle chain on her right ankle and nice ass pie—at first. She loved her some Roger—me. From the start, we hit it off, and from the start, we were at the hotel doing the nasty—she was my kind of girl. During sex, on the first night and in the second hour, she was asking me if I loved her. Me being the kind of guy I am and in the middle of sex said, "Sure, baby. I love you. I love you so much." I should have known right then; I should have seen the writing on the wall. But sex will do that to a guy and it's so close to love you think it is. So, you stay.

After a while, little things start distinguishing the girl from my first love. She's starting to change, where the other stopped, this one started.

"Roger, where you going? Hold on I'll go with you. Are you mad at me Roger? Come on in this bedroom and I'll fix everything. Roger, I love you so much I'll never let you go."

One day, she came back from lunch from with a few of her friends and told me they saw my car in the park with a strange lady in it. They weren't sure but they were pretty sure it was me. "You want to tell me who the lady was, Roger? Do I know her?" I tried to tell her that there was no such lady and I wasn't in the park on the day her friends said I was—they were mistaken. "I hope so, Roger, because if I ever found out it was true, I think I'd have to hurt you."

"Hey, where'd that come from?" I said. "Where'd the love go?"

There comes a time when you can look in your woman's face and tell when she's serious—this was one of those times that you don't won't to be right, hoping you're wrong but you don't think so. I think the night she stabbed me in the back did it for me.

I was home and had just finished 12 hours at the plant, had a couple of drinks, and a TV dinner and hit the sack. Twelve hours come and go quickly. This was Lottie's night out with the girls— their get down night, as they called it. She came in stumbling a little after one and went into the kitchen and didn't even take her clothes off. From the kitchen, she came into the bedroom. I was lying on my stomach with my arms above my head, with the covers halfway down my back. That's when she did it—she put the steak knife in my back and I screamed. If you ever heard the saying "screamed like a little bitch", that was me.

Before the medics came, she had stabbed me five more times before she came to her senses and called 911.

I found out later that she had been listening to her friends again and that the alcohol triggered her. If I didn't know before, I knew then that the bitch was crazy. She went to jail for six months and I quit my job, packed my stuff and moved out of the house. Not only did I move out of the house, but I moved out of town and the state. It was close to three years before I had another relationship. When I needed some drawls, I found myself an upscale prostitute, paid her the going price, and took my ass back home. It worked out fine! I ran into one of her friends a few years later and she told me that Lottie had since remarried an upstanding real estate developer and a while after, the guy was found murdered.

"Lottie ended up a rich woman. Every time I would see her, all she would talk about was you," she said. "I think she still loves you."

"Well, do me a favor," I said. "Don't mention you saw me."

"Where are you staying now?" she asked.

"Baltimore," I said. There was no way in hell I was going to tell her where I really lived.

I was in Florida, on the beach, watching all the bikini sweeties. I was on vacation and feeling pretty good—no worries! No worries whatsoever. I was under an umbrella with a cooler, and a six pack of beer and two wine coolers in it. Men and women were surfboarding, playing volleyball, and whatever else you do on a beach. Florida has some of the most beautiful women in the world from all nationalities. Most were wearing bikinis of all kinds. Some looked like they had no bikinis at all—just G-strings. They could have just taken those off, for all the good they did.

I don't know, I've always liked having something for the imagination. A bunch of nude women walking around—what's the fun in that? A while later, a few girls were playing grab ass and one failed where I was laying and she just laid there. "Are you all right?" I asked. I could see she was about 19 years old. Her skin was golden brown and she had on a bikini that just wouldn't quit. Her bottoms were almost nonexistent and a halter that just covered her nipples. I'd say a little bit of all right.

"Yes, I'm okay," she said. "I think the sun is trying to get to me." At that moment, her friends came over and asked about her condition and she told them about getting too much sun. "I just need to lay here a few minutes, is that okay?" she asked.

"Sure," I said. "Get further underneath the umbrella. I've got a few drinks here can I offer you anything?" She took one of the wine coolers and told me she and her friends were there getting over man troubles—at least two of them were anyway. It seems like the boys she gets, one girl can't seem to satisfy them so we or I couldn't go with that so I walked. So, I'm here to wash away the past. What about you?"

"Oh, you don't want to hear about me," I said. "Your story pales compared to mine. But then, I am quite a few years older than you."

"Go ahead and tell me, it may make me feel better. I sure can't feel any worse," she said.

So, I told her everything from my first love to the last one stabbing me in the back. By the time I'd finished, she'd finish her second wine cooler and two of my beers.

"Damn," she said. "My story is weak compared to yours. I think I'll be all right now. Have you found another woman yet?"

"No, I haven't. You know, I don't even know your name," I said.

"Lottie," she said. "My name is Lottie."

One never knows who one will see on their travels. If you travel far enough and long enough, you'll see someone who knows someone that you know. You'll even see some people that look like someone you know. After all, they say everyone has a double somewhere. I remember once I was coming out of the library and a female cop stopped me, asked for my identification—which I gave to her—and we both went our separate ways. I wouldn't have thought much of it except that she had stopped me twice before in the last six months. I gave her the same driver's license I always carry, plus my Veterans Administration card with my photo. I haven't grown any and haven't put on that much weight. So, I asked her why she was stopping me so much, and told her that I must remind her of someone. Or maybe she was just harassing me, or trying to hit on me. I didn't say that to her, but I thought it. Or is it because I'm black? I never received an answer to any one of those questions. I'd like to thank it's because I remind her of someone, probably from the wanted posters—we all look alike they say.

Eventually, I found another mate and I mean that, a mate! Not too many issues. We could talk about different things—the news, PBS, and the history channels. Shows like Alaska, Fishing, American Greed, and Lockup—those are my shows. Don't get me wrong, we have our private shows that we like, and that's why we have two TVs.

Love was lost years ago, but I have found a friend. Even though we have separate bedrooms, we manage to find time for sex and a decent conversation. It's not the end of the line, not quite! Not yet!

It won't take long before your kids will find you. You've done all you can for them and they still hang around. Money is number one or advice that they never follow anyway. Whoever said that at eighteen, they're on their own, get their own family, and a life. Whoever said that must not have any kids. The reality is that your kids will be

with you for the rest of your life. Your life is their
life. If they have troubles, then you have troubles.
If they have troubles with their kids, then you
have trouble with their kids. It never seems to
end. I figured that when I finished with my first
love, that would be the end of story. But no, I still
must deal with her through the kids. Hey, I love
my kids just like any other father, I just don't want
them hanging around all the time. Same thing with
grandkids. My son, I hate to say, was never like
me. Of course, he has his good side and his bad
side. The good side is that he fell in love at an
early age, just like me, and he stayed with the girl
longer then I thought he would. Maybe that's
because that was his first love. I don't mean the
first girl he's screwed but the first girl he cared
enough about to stay with. And I don't mean it like
that, he's stayed with a lot of girls and they let
him. They paid. Cell phones, they bought them and
paid the note every month. Food, car notes, car
insurance, and utilities. You name it! Fucked him

up! And on top of that, his mother's giving him more money all the time. Right now, he has more than one mother. Right now, he is no good for no woman. Sometimes, I have to put my head down between my legs when I'm talking to him because I can't believe what's coming out of his mouth. Now, it's about love. I knew it was coming. "I don't think she loves me. I don't think she cares," he says. "I think I'm gonna leave her."

"Let's see," I said. "You've been with the girl almost five years now. She bore you two children. The longest you ever held a job was less than six months. You're always talking about what she's not bringing to the table, even though she's the only one with a job. What's hers is yours and what's yours is yours. Are we living in the same world? It can't be possible that you are my son, where did I go wrong? Then, you'll say shit to me like 'you never did anything for me' and then I bring up the bike I bought you at Christmas time, a lot of bikes really. The clothes that you wore and the lights that came on to run that TV in your room that I paid for. The 12 and 18 hour shifts I worked at a job I hated. No, I won't bring that up, I won't tell you the many times I wanted to leave home but didn't because I had a family to feed. A man just doesn't up and leave because things are not going his way at the time. But you can believe a lot of men have thought about doing just that, and women. And one other thing, you're always calling your mama, mama my ass! I saw her in there packing her own bags one night. I could tell you all those things but I won't because I'm your dad and I don't want to hurt you. Now, you have your own family, your own standards and values, what are you gonna do? Years from now, what will your kids be saying about you? Where will you tell them you were when they needed you? Think hard and long what you want to do. Real love only comes around once, the others are just imitations. But, then there's nothing wrong with that except you'll never find real love again."

"But dad," he said, "what about Rudolph? He's been married five times. You can't tell me he hasn't found love again."

"Yes," I said. "Again and again and again. Don't equate sex with love. If you had kept up with him in the tabloids, you would've found out that he's been trying to get his first love back for years but she's moved on. Son, go home! Kick your wife in the ass, and hug your kids if that's what it takes. Find yourself a job, keep it and live happily ever after. But then, that's another story."

September 16, 2010

My friend passed away today. The passing wasn't like any other I've ever known, like my mother's or my grandmother's, where the hurt went straight down to my very soul, thinking how they could just leave like that, even though they've been preparing me all my life for such an event. Regardless, I was still devastated. For a parent, a kid's death is the worst thing that could happen to you in your life, then, there is the second worst thing, like losing my best friend, Herbert, I'll surely miss him.

Pussy Whipped

"2 Sweet, 2 Sweet, you're just 2 Sweet. You bob, dance and weave just like a regular Mohammed Ali." That's what the sportswriters use to say about Robert Jeremy the third. Aka, 2 Sweet Jennings. In his day, he was one of the best-known welterweights around, but he just had one obsession—the ladies. Each night, before a fight, he was known to fight poorly if he spent the previous night or had sex, never failed. He said, he just didn't care about winning or losing, he was going to get some. He could have been a champion but today, he's working at Champion Carwash.

People still come by the car wash occasionally to ask him for autographs and chant the phrase, "2 Sweet, 2 Sweet, you just 2 Sweet. You bob, dance and weave just like Mohammed Ali." They once said a spectator threw a $20 bill into the ring, you stopped the fight to pick it up and found out that it wasn't real. 2 sweet would walk down the street even though he had two new cars and the people would ask him why he walked when he could ride. His reply was, "You see all these ladies around me? I can't get all of them in my car, nor can I sign autographs, nor can I show off this new herringbone suit and Stetson shoes, herringbone fedora, the tie pin and diamond watch and rings. I'll ride when the time comes but right now, I'm enjoying the moment."

Sweet won his last five fights by technical knockouts (TKO) and was about to get a shot at the title. His manager told him, "All you have to do is keep doing what you're doing and you'll be on top of the mountain. Just stay away from the ladies during fight time." 2 Sweet agreed but he was lying. With all the beauties out there, they wanted him to just pass them up? he wasn't a fool.

During one fight, 2 Sweet was put on the canvas. A guy that had no reason being in the same ring with 2 Sweet, but there 2 Sweet was, on his ass in the middle of the ring. The bell saved him that time, and he was more embarrassed than anything. However, he came back and knocked the guy out in the very next round.

They found out later that 2 Sweet had two girls in his room the night before, after the party. 2 Sweet felt that the guy he was fighting was such a pushover and hadn't had that many fights, that he didn't need to prepare and as a result, almost lost the fight and a shot at the title. That should have been a wake-up call for 2 Sweet, and it was for a while. The next three fights went on without a hitch, putting the men away 1, 2, 3. During the last fight, he picked up a little honey but at two in the morning, he told her she had to go. He felt that was good. He put the guy away in four rounds that night, although his manager told him he should have done it in two.

The subject around "pussy whipped" came up and his manager tried to explain it to him. "You can't handle it," his manager said. "You can get all the pussy you want after the fight, but not before. You don't know when to stop, like an alcoholic, you can't stop at just one. When all other normal men stop at 2 or 3 nuts, you have to go above and beyond. Night gone, strength gone and your ass is gone. Pussy whipped! Then, you wake up the next morning, and try to do some more. Even the girl has had enough by that time. You have to stop or at least scale-down. You know, 2 Sweet," he said, "you may need some help. I've heard of guys like you that never get enough. There's a clinic that I've heard of that's for guys just like you."

A few weeks later, 2 Sweet's manager had convinced him to enroll in North Texas Sex Clinic, a 30-day course, with follow-up outside the clinic.

"Mr. Jennings, do you want to tell us your story? How did you get here?" The therapist said amid a group of five individuals who were all sex addicts.

"Well, Miss Edwards, it's like this: I love sex, and I always have. I just can't seem to get enough, I'm addicted. I've made love to just about every girl I know, my girl's girlfriends, my boyfriend's girlfriends, and their relatives. I've screwed everyone that's been close to me."

"With you being who you are, there should be plenty of women out there for you. Why do you need your friend's women?"

"Because, Ms. Edwards, I'm addicted. I can make love twelve hours a day and I don't know how in the hell I got this way, that's why I'm here. Don't get me wrong, I love making love but I also hate it."

"What do you think is going to eventually happen to you, Mr. Jennings, if you continue on this road?"

"Oh, I don't know. I'll probably lose everything I have. The shot at the title, the money, the cars, the clothes and women."

"You think that will force you to stop?"

"No, not really. There'll always be women out there that want sex. Maybe not as many as now because I'm a celebrity, but some."

Within a week, 2 Sweet had sex with his therapist and two others and was kicked out of the program with the three therapists following.

During his next fight, his opponent put him down twice—one in the second round and again in the fourth. But again, 2 Sweet returned from both knockdowns to win on a decision. 2 Sweet was starting to get hurt more now. Before, he could bob and weave and slip punches, but it was getting harder to do so now, and it was getting harder and harder to recuperate after each fight. Every time he had a close fight like that, his fight for the title moved further away. 2 Sweet was still popular, but his manager could see he was losing it. He tried everything he could, but there was only so much he could do. 2 Sweet's dick had taken control over him and his manager felt there was no way back. The next three fights were; win, decision and a draw. The shot at the title was withdrawn. "Who would want to pay to see 2 Sweet the champ now?"

The end came on a Saturday night. 2 Sweet was not the headliner but the third on the ticket. When 2 Sweet walked into the ring, he didn't look like the same old 2 Sweet. The swagger was gone, and he didn't jump over the top ropes on entering the ring. The dancing around wasn't there; it just wasn't 2 Sweet. But then, no one knew about the woman in his hotel room that had stayed with him until 5 that morning, and he calling another up at two that afternoon.

The bell rang for round one, and 2 Sweet almost ran out to the middle of the ring. He looked like the 2 Sweet of old, until that first punch was thrown and the next twenty-five after that, all by his opponent. They had to carry 2 Sweet out on a stretcher that night.

A week later, sweet was back at the gym and told his manager he was back and ready to train. His manager gave him the bad news that the ride was over and he'd have to find something else to do. 2 Sweet took that like he took everything else that's happened to him in his life. The fast cars, the autographs, the clothes and the women were no longer available to him. But being 2 Sweet, he said, "Okay, what you guys waiting on, send that next car through."

Eddie J. Martin